Bernard, Me, and the Letter B

Alphabet Friends

by Cynthia Klingel and Robert B. Noyed

The Child's World

The Child's World

Published in the United States of America
by The Child's World®
P.O. Box 326
Chanhassen, MN 55317-0326
800-599-READ
www.childsworld.com

The Child's World®: Mary Berendes, Publishing Director

Editorial Directions, Inc.: E. Russell Primm, Editorial
Director; Emily Dolbear, Line Editor; Ruth Martin,
Editorial Assistant; Linda S. Koutris, Photo Researcher
and Selector

Photographs ©: Corbis: Cover & 21, 9; William Hart/
Stone/Getty Images: 10; Lawrence Manning/Corbis:
13; Davis Barber/PhotoEdit: 14; Myrleen Ferguson
Cate/PhotoEdit: 17; Spencer Grant: 18.

Library of Congress Cataloging-in-Publication Data
Klingel, Cynthia Fitterer.
  Bernard, me, and the letter B / by Cynthia Klingel
and Robert B. Noyed.
     p. cm. — (Alphabet readers)
Summary: A simple story about a boy named Bernard
and his younger brother introduces the letter "b".
  ISBN 1-59296-092-8 (alk. paper)
  [1. Brothers—Fiction. 2. Alphabet.] I. Noyed, Robert B.
II. Title. III. Series.
  PZ7.K6798Be 2003
  [E]—dc21   2003006490

Note to parents and educators:
The first skill children acquire before
becoming successful readers is individual
letter recognition. The Alphabet Friends
series has been created with the needs of
young learners in mind. Each engaging book
begins by showing the difference between
the capital letter and the lowercase letter.
In each of the books on the vowels and the
consonants c and g, children are introduced
to the different sounds that the letter can
make. Finally, children see that the letters can
be found at the beginning of a word, in the
middle of a word, and in most cases, at the
end of a word.

Following the introduction, children
meet their Alphabet Friends. The friend in
each story encounters many words that
include the featured letter of that book.
Each noun that begins with the title letter is
highlighted in red with the initial letter of the
word in bold. Above the word is a rebus
drawing that establishes a strong picture cue.

At the end of each book, we have
included three words lists. Can your young
learners find all the words in each book with
the title letter in them?

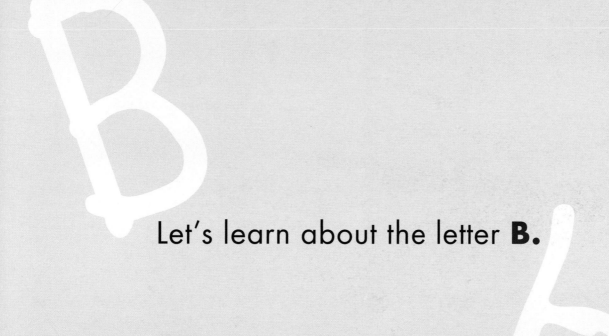

Let's learn about the letter **B.**

The letter **B** can look like this: **B.**

The letter **B** can also look like this: **b.**

The letter **b** can be at the beginning of a word, like balloon.

balloon

The letter **b** can be in the middle of a word, like jellybeans.

jelly**b**eans

The letter **b** can be at the
end of a word, like cab.

ca**b**

I have a **b**rother named **B**ernard. He is

my big **b**rother. He was born before me.

Bernard is my best friend. I share

a room with **B**ernard. We have

bunk **b**eds.

Bernard and I like to play **b**aseball

together. I use his **b**at to hit the **b**aseball.

Bernard lets me ride his **b**ike. He has

a black and silver **b**ike. I need **B**ernard

to boost me onto the **b**ike.

Bernard takes me to the **b**each. I love to

be at the **b**each. We splash in the water.

Bernard buys me a balloon. He

buys the biggest balloon. The balloon

is bright blue.

Bernard keeps me busy. I love my

brother **B**ernard. He is my best friend.

Fun Facts

 The **b**alloons in this story are the kind you see at birthday parties. But did you know that **b**alloons have many different uses? For example, scientists use a certain kind of **b**alloon to collect information about the weather. And some very large **b**alloons are made so that you can ride in a basket underneath them!

 Baseball is the name of both a popular game and the ball used to play that game. A **b**aseball is small and hard and weighs about 5 ounces (142 g). That means it's lighter than this book! China makes about 80 percent of the world's **b**aseballs.

 The word *bike* is short for *bicycle,* or sometimes *motorcycle.* Bicycles used to be an extremely popular way to travel. When the automobile was invented, people stopped buying as many **b**ikes. They became popular with kids, though, and today both adults and children enjoy riding bicycles.

To Read More

About the Letter B
Albee, Sarah, and Joe Mathieu (illustrator). *Brought to You by the Letter B*. New York: Random House, 2000.
Flanagan, Alice K. *I Like Bugs: The Sound of B*. Chanhassen, Minn.: The Child's World, 2000.

About Balloons
Faulkner, Keith, and Rory Tyger (illustrator). *Pop Went Another Balloon*. New York: Dutton, 2003.
Inkpen, Mick. *Blue Balloon*. Boston: Little, Brown, 1990.

About Baseball
Buckley, Jim. *Baseball 1-2-3*. New York: Kindersley Publishing, 2001.
Gibbons, Gail. *My Baseball Book*. New York: HarperCollins, 2000.

About Bikes
Barrett, John E. (photographer). *Big Enough for a Bike*. New York: Random House, 2002.
Blackstone, Stella, and Debbie Harter (illustrator). *Bear on a Bike*. Cambridge, Mass.: Barefoot Books, 2000.

Words with B

Words with **B** at the Beginning

balloon
baseball
bat
be
beach
before
beginning
Bernard
best
big
biggest
bike
black
blue
boost
born
bright
brother
bunk beds
busy
buys

Words with **B** in the Middle

about
baseball
jellybeans

Words with **B** at the End

cab

About the Authors

Cynthia Klingel has worked as a high school English teacher and an elementary teacher. She is currently the curriculum director for a Minnesota school district. Cynthia Klingel lives with her family in Mankato, Minnesota.

Robert B. Noyed started his career as a newspaper reporter. Since then, he has worked in communications and public relations for a Minnesota school district for more than fourteen years. Robert B. Noyed lives with his family in Brooklyn Center, Minnesota.